A Kiss
Like This

Catherine &
Laurence Anholt

BARRON'S

When Little Cub was born,
Big Golden Lion just
couldn't stop kissing him.

"GRRRR!" he growled. "You're the most kissable cub in the world."

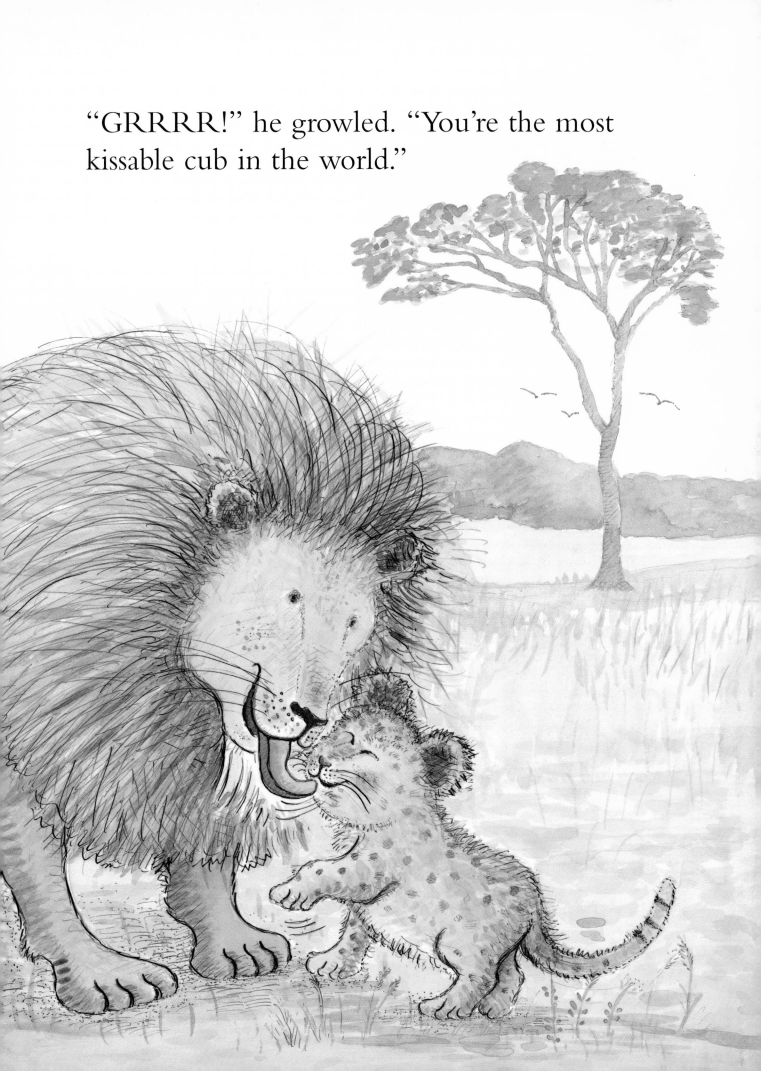

Big Golden Lion kissed Little Cub behind his prickly ears . . . *just like this.*

And Little Cub giggled.

He kissed Little Cub on the end of his small pink nose . . . *just like this.*

And Little Cub wriggled.

He kissed Little Cub right on his warm fat
tummy and blew a raspberry on his
belly button . . .

. . . *just like this.*

And Little Cub giggled and wriggled and
jiggled.

In the golden evening
sunshine, Little Cub played outside.

Everyone who passed by and saw Little Cub
wanted to kiss him too.

They just couldn't help it.

Along came Jumpy Monkey

and gave Little Cub a tickly
monkey kiss behind his
prickly ears,

on the end of his small pink nose

and right in the middle of his warm fat tummy . . .

. . . *just like this.*

And Little Cub giggled and wriggled and jiggled.

Along came Squawky Parrot

and gave Little Cub a pecky
parrot kiss behind his
prickly ears,

on the end of his
small pink nose

and right in the middle of his warm fat
tummy . . .

. . . *just like this.*

And Little Cub giggled and wriggled and
jiggled even more.

Along came
Big Fat Rhino

and gave Little Cub a
nuzzling nosy rhino
kiss behind his
prickly ears,

on the end of his
small pink nose

and right in the middle of his warm fat
tummy . . .

. . . *just like this.*

And Little Cub giggled and wriggled and
jiggled all over again.

Along came Slippery Snake

and gave Little Cub a
s-s-slow hiss-s-sing
s-s-snake kiss-s-s
behind his prickly
ears-s-s,

on the end of his
small pink nos-s-se

and right in the middle of his warm fat
tummy . . .

. . . *just like this-s-s.*

And Little Cub giggled and wriggled and
jiggled even more than before.

Along came
Old Gray Elephant

and gave Little Cub a
slurpy sloppy elephant
kiss behind his
prickly ears,

on the end of his
small pink nose

and right in the middle of his warm fat
tummy . . .

. . . *just like this.*

And Little Cub giggled and wriggled and
jiggled more than ever.

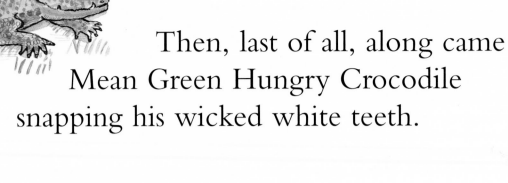

Then, last of all, along came Mean Green Hungry Crocodile snapping his wicked white teeth.

He saw Little Cub playing in the golden evening sunshine.

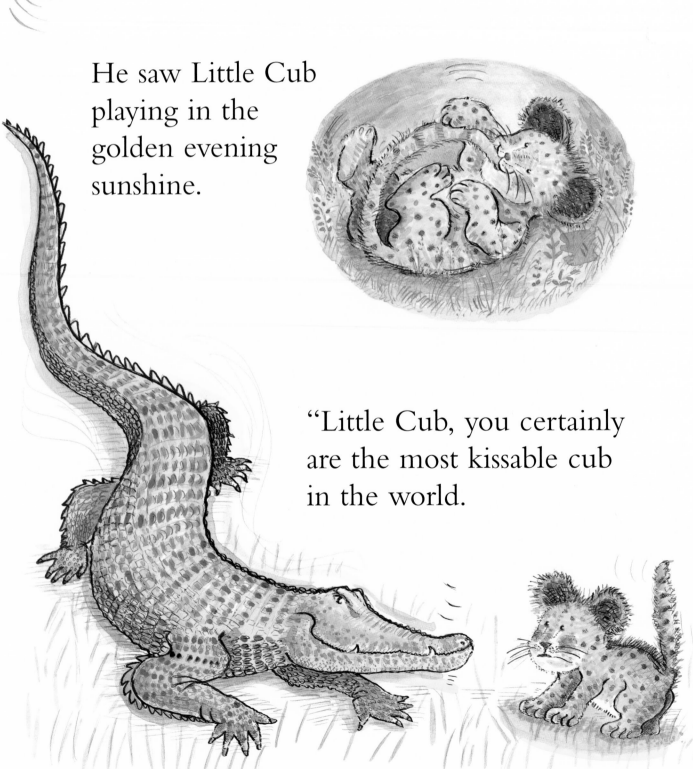

"Little Cub, you certainly are the most kissable cub in the world.

"Come over here and I will give you a
snippy snappy crocodile kiss."

But Little Cub didn't want a snippy snappy crocodile kiss at all. And he began to cry.

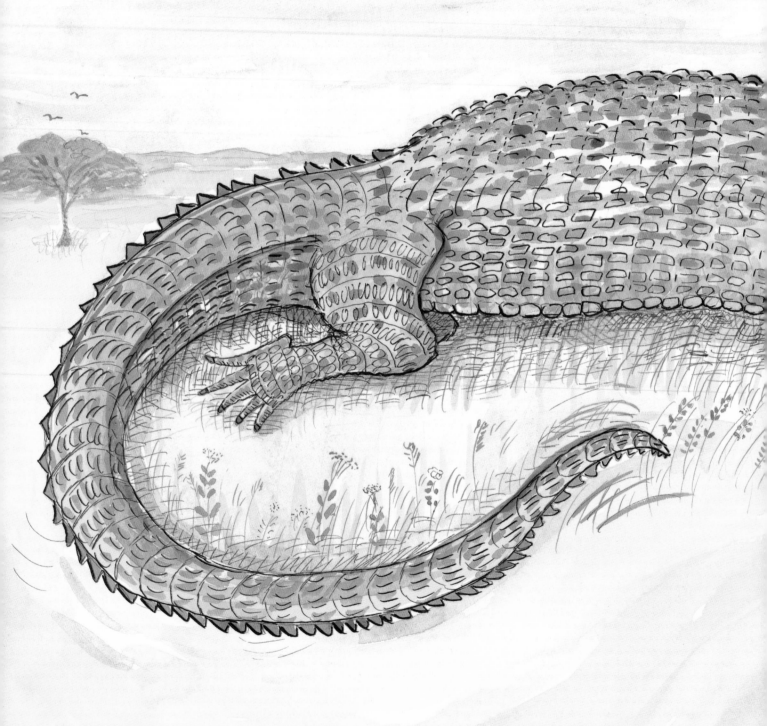

Mean Green Hungry Crocodile opened
his mean green hungry mouth and showed
all his wicked white crocodile teeth . . .

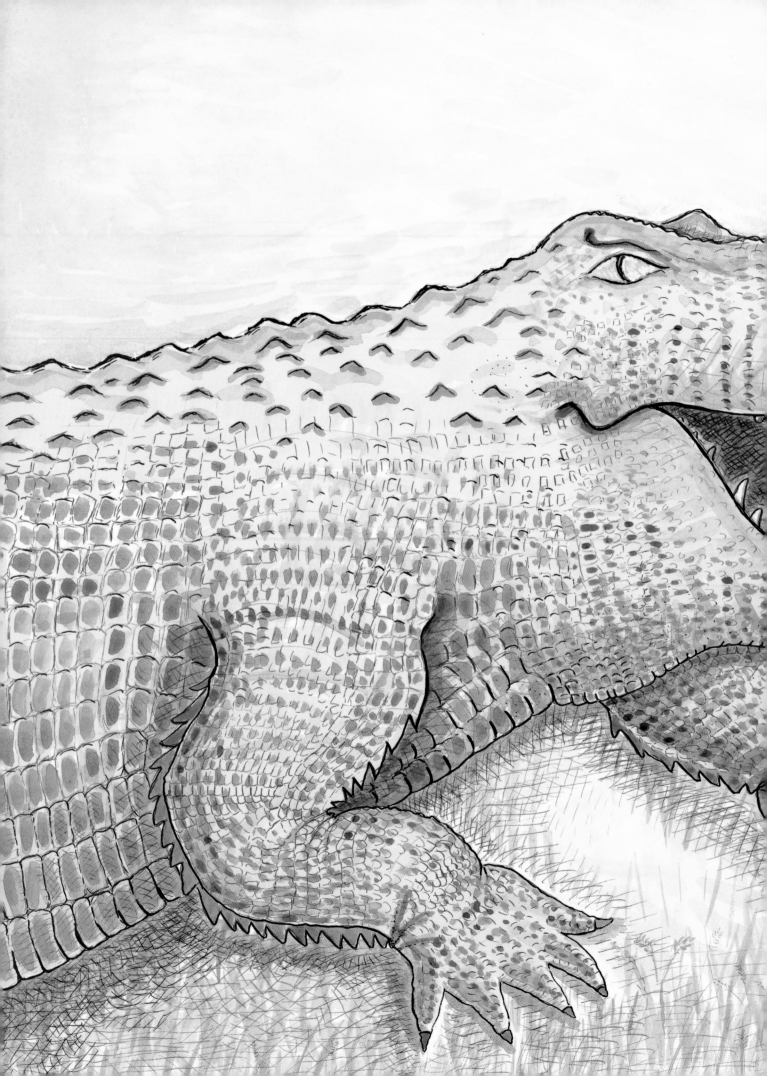

. . . JUST LIKE THIS!

Quick as a flash, along came Big Golden
Lion and **ROARED** a Big
Golden Lion **ROAR** until Mean Green
Hungry Crocodile turned and ran away.

Big Golden Lion carried Little Cub back to their safe warm home and tucked him into his safe warm bed.

Then Big Golden Lion stretched himself. "Listen, Little Cub," he said.

"There's nothing better than a tickly monkey kiss – when you're a tiny monkey.

"And a parrot peck is perfect – when you're a baby parrot.

"No one loves a rhino nuzzle quite like a newborn rhino.

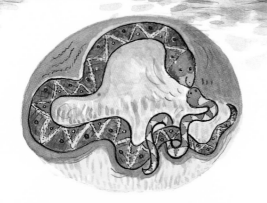

"A s-s-snake kiss-s-s is especially nic-c-ce – when you're a baby snake.

"And you can't have too many elephant kisses – when you're a little elephant.

"And *even* snippy snappy baby crocodiles love snippy snappy kisses."

"But," said Big Golden Lion, yawning, "when you're a sleepy Little Lion Cub, there's only one thing in the whole wide world that's completely, exactly right.

"And that's . . .

"...a **HUGE GREAT**
Big Golden Lion kiss . . .

"*...just like this!*"

For Jill Anholt
with a kiss like this

First edition for the United States
published 1997 by Barron's Educational Series, Inc.

First published in Great Britain by Hamish Hamilton Ltd, a subsidiary of the Penguin
Group, Penguin Books Ltd, 27 Wrights Lane, London W8 5TZ, England

Text copyright (c) Laurence Anholt, 1997
Illustrations copyright (c) Catherine Anholt, 1997

All inquiries should be addressed to:

Barron's Educational Series, Inc.
250 Wireless Boulevard
Hauppauge, New York 11788

ISBN 0-7641-5068-5

Library of Congress Catalog Card Number: 97-16452

Printed in Singapore

Library of Congress Cataloging-in-Publication Data

Anholt, Catherine.
    A kiss like this / Catherine & Laurence Anholt. — 1st ed.
        p.   cm.
    "First published in Great Britain by Hamish Hamilton Ltd"—T.p.
verso.
    Summary: Little Cub enjoys the kisses of Big Golden Lion, as well
as those of other animals, until Mean Green Hungry Crocodile
tries to kiss him.
    ISBN 0-7641-5068-5
    [1. Lions—Fiction.   2. Animals—Fiction.]   I. Anholt, Laurence.
II. Title.
PZ7.A5863Ki   1997
[E]—dc21   97-16452
                                                                    CIP
                                                                    AC